CW00418606

Beyond Our Yesterdays

A Novella by

Simon Cook

If you enjoyed reading this,
please pass it onto a friend or family member,
donate it to a charity bookshop
or return it to a telephone box book community.
I'd love to see where this book travels to,
you can email a picture to simoncookbooks@gmail.com

For my family.

Acknowledgements

A sincere thank you goes out to Simon J. Curd, the exceptionally talented artist behind the mesmerizing cover of my book. With his remarkable skill and deep understanding of my vision, he effortlessly brought it to life.

I am immensely grateful to my editor and friend, Rich Lee, whose guidance, and support helped me unearth the depths of the story and navigate the necessary changes, allowing the book to reach its full potential.

Also, I express my deepest appreciation to my wife for her unwavering support, constant encouragement, and invaluable time dedicated to reading the numerous rewrites that accompanied our journey towards the completion of this book.

And lastly, I extend my gratitude to you, dear reader, for embarking on this literary journey with me and investing your time in reading my debut novella.

It means the world to me, and I eagerly anticipate the opportunity to share more captivating stories with you in the future.

Prologue

Tuesday morning felt like any other for Samantha Greene of Cheswick, a suburb of London. The serene symphony of birds filled the air, their melodious songs gently awakening Samantha from her slumber. The early morning commuters hurried past her window, their footsteps creating a rhythmic beat on the pavement below.

Before starting her day, Samantha had a comforting routine. Sitting in her kitchen, she enjoyed a cup of freshly brewed coffee and a bowl of cereal by the open window, taking in the sights and sounds of the bustling main street. The aroma of coffee filled the air, adding a pleasant energy to the room. She relished each spoonful of cereal, enjoying the satisfying crunch and the coolness of the milk. It was a simple pleasure that brought her joy.

She reached for her phone, its screen illuminating her face as she swiftly skimmed through the morning news stories, taking note of the headlines and glancing at any articles that caught her attention. With a quick tap, she checked the weather forecast for the day, ensuring she was prepared for whatever conditions awaited her outside. A sense of relief washed over her as she confirmed that the trains on her morning commute remained unaffected by the recent staffing strikes. Placing the phone back on the table, she took another spoonful of her cereal.

This peaceful moment provided Samantha with a chance to observe the flow of life outside her window. The vibrant tapestry of humanity unfolded before her eyes. Pedestrians scurried along the sidewalk, their faces reflecting a blend of determination and anticipation. Cars and buses charged past, their engines humming in unison, creating a symphony of urban life.

However, on this day, amidst the chorus of daily routines, an unexpected disruption shattered the tranquility. As Samantha took another mouthful of cereal, she suddenly experienced a jolt of discomfort. A sharpness pierced through her chest, leaving her momentarily breathless. Startled, she dropped her spoon, instinctively reaching for her coffee. The liquid cascaded down her throat, an attempt to alleviate the discomfort she felt.

But the ache persisted, intensifying with each passing moment. Panic seized her as she struggled to draw in a full breath. In a desperate attempt to fill her lungs, she gasped for air, but it eluded her. The world around her seemed to fade into a haze as the suffocation stole her vision. From the edge of her fading consciousness, Samantha dimly registered a distant cacophony of screams.

It was a chorus of fear, an unsettling sound that pierced the veil of silence that had descended upon the once-bustling city. And then, an eerie stillness settled upon London, as if the very essence of life had been muted.

Even the birds ceased their music, their songs silenced. As the suffocating darkness closed in on Samantha, her body slumped forward, her weakened form crumpling onto the table. Her awareness diminished, slipping away like a waning tide, as her last remnants of life ebbed away.

The city stood silent, witnessing an inexplicable tragedy unfold.

Chapter 1

Ethan Turner's journey from a tumultuous upbringing to a compassionate child psychologist and bar manager in Greenfield, Franklin County, USA, shaped his character in profound ways.

Born Wednesday 17th September 1997, at Springfield Medical Centre, he entered the world with uncertainty, abandoned by his birth parents and thrust into the foster care system. The constant shuffling from one home to another, and even a period spent living on the streets, instilled in him a resilience that would eventually break the cycle of adversity.

Despite the challenges he faced, Ethan found purpose in the small town of Greenfield, Massachusetts, situated within Pioneer Valley across the Connecticut River. Known for its rich history and ties to the colonial era, Greenfield preserves its agricultural and industrial roots while nurturing a small yet strong, close-knit community.

Determined to make a difference in his adult life, he pursued night schooling, immersing himself in the study of child psychology.

His firm commitment led him to pursue a diploma in behavioral science, excelling in his assignments with an intelligence that displayed exceptional insight and empathy for the human condition.

With his new-found knowledge, passion, and drive to help others he was brought in on an apprenticeship at a local free practice in Greenfields, studying alongside their seasoned practitioners. The practice was a county-funded building situated on Silver Street, dedicated to helping children struggling both within the area and across the river to nearby towns.

The Silver Street team became a pillar of support for those in need, offering guidance and understanding to young minds navigating the complexities of life.

Because he couldn't live on the rewards of such endeavors alone, Ethan also managed a local bar five nights a week, seamlessly blending his love for connecting with people and his genuine desire to help others.

It was at the nostalgic Northfield Drive-In Theatre that fate intervened, intertwining Ethan's life with that of Nicole's. As the projection flickered on the silver screen, Nicole Clark arrived in her father's beloved blue 1985 Ford Mustang convertible, pulling up alongside Ethan and his friend Marcus in his police patrol car.

Nicole, who was in her car with friends, leaned out of

the window and greeted them. "Evening, officers," she said with a warm smile and sparkle in her eyes.

Marcus returned the smile across the patrol car, while Ethan, sitting in the passenger seat, leaned out to speak to her.

"Good evening," Ethan said with a playfully charming voice. "I may not be a cop," he paused for a mischievous moment, "but if you like a man in uniform, I don't look bad in an apron."

Nicole's laughter erupted at the perfect moment during a quiet part in the movie, drawing everyone's attention to the patrol car.

Ethan blushed slightly but quickly regained his composure, offering a witty response. "How about you join me for dinner one evening this week, and I'll demonstrate?" he suggested, a playful grin spreading across his face.

Impressed by his confidence, Nicole gladly accepted the invitation. Ethan did indeed look good in an apron and proved to be a skilled cook as well. As the night drew to a close, he displayed his gentlemanly demeanor by walking Nicole to her parents' house, which was only a few blocks away. This scored top marks for a first date.

And so, their journey together began. Their initial dinner date led to trips to the movies and shared enjoyment of the exploration of the great outdoors.

Two years later, surrounded by their loved ones, Ethan and Nicole stood before the altar of the Trinitarian Congregational Church across the river in Northfield, where they first met, pledging their love and commitment to one another.

With the wisdom and strength that came from overcoming the trials of his youth, Ethan Turner stood tall and proud in his late twenties. His clean-shaven face and short, dark hair spoke of determination and purpose, a reflection of the resilient and compassionate man he had become.

Despite the memories of his tough upbringing and hard times spent on the streets of Springfield, he had managed to break free from their grasp, defying the odds that had ensnared many others in a cycle of despair.

His athletic physique spoke of a life lived in motion, his body a testament to the perseverance that had carried him through the toughest of times. Every step he took, every hurdle he overcame, reflected his determination to rise above his circumstances and forge a path of his own.

Ethan possessed an innate ability to seek out the flickers of light in even the darkest corners of the world. With unremitting optimism, he believed that change was possible, not only within oneself but also in the hearts and minds of others. He saw the potential for transformation in people and their environments, and he was determined in his commitment to inspire that change.

Together, Ethan and Nicole cherished the love they shared, recognizing that true happiness could not be bought with material possessions.

Their two-bedroom house on Hope Street, which was once part of an old manor that had been converted into three properties, became their sanctuary. Although it required extensive renovation, the couple found beauty in the process of transforming it into a cozy haven. The west wing, which now belonged to them, left open plan for the new owners to divide however suited their needs. The kitchen, tucked at the back, offered a glimpse of their shared vision of a warm and inviting home. The main downstairs space, bathed in natural light streaming through large windows, served as a space of relaxation.

Upstairs, they had decided on a more conventional layout, with two large bedrooms and a small home office for Nicole. Her father, a retired Ford salesperson with a knack for DIY projects, lent a helping hand in constructing the plasterboard walls that provided privacy and structure to their home. The bathroom remained a spacious canvas, awaiting their creative touch and personalized design.

Nicole ran her small online business with friends from

Greenfield, selling office supplies in Pioneer Valley.

She reveled in the freedom of working from the comfort of their home since the 2020 coronavirus pandemic had reshaped the landscape of businesses.

Despite growing up in the digital era, Ethan developed a deep affection for vinyl records.

He meticulously curated his collection with hidden gems and forgotten classics acquired mainly from thrift stores over the years. Often, he would come across names or initials scribbled in the corners of the album covers, each album carrying its own story and serving as a bridge between the past and the present. The worn sleeves and weathered edges of the album covers bore witness to decades of love and enjoyment. To Ethan, these marks served as a reminder that music has the power to transcend time and connect people across generations. In the evenings, bathed in the soft glow of antique lamps, Ethan would sit among his vinyl collection, savoring the melodies that filled the air. The music transported him to a different time and place, evoking emotions, and memories that only the power of music could conjure.

Nicole Turner, a tall and slender woman, possessed a magnetic presence that radiated an irresistible charm. With her curvaceous figure and flowing brunette curls framing her captivating, emerald eyes, she exuded an aura of elegance and grace.

Raised in a large and supportive family, she carried with her the values instilled by her father, who had been her rock of support throughout her life.

Nicole's longing to become a mother began to permeate every aspect of her being. It was a deep, primal desire that tugged at her heartstrings with every passing day.

Her conversations with friends often revolved around the joys and challenges of parenthood, and she would find herself caught in a bittersweet mix of excitement and wistfulness as she witnessed the joy radiating from parents and their children.

In their home, Ethan and Nicole had prepared a warm and nurturing environment, filled with love and support. Their home, bathed with sunlight and gentle colors, seemed to yearn for the pitter-patter of little feet and the laughter of a child. The walls, painted in hues of soft pastels, whispered secrets of dreams yet to be fulfilled.

Despite their optimism and belief that their journey to parenthood would unfold in due course, there were moments when doubt would creep into their hearts. They would cast fleeting glances at one another, searching for reassurance in the depths of each other's eyes, silently questioning if their dream would ever materialize.

At times, the weight of their unfulfilled desire would

be punctuated by a sudden ache of longing. On quiet evenings, they would find comfort in each other's arms, their whispers of encouragement and gentle touches serving as reminders that they were on this adventure together, bound by an unbreakable love and shared hope for what lay ahead.

Amid their longing, they continued to build a life that would one day welcome their greatest joy.

Their bond grew stronger, their love deepened, and they immersed themselves in the beauty of the present, finding gratitude in the small miracles that surrounded them.

Ethan and Nicole's optimism and enduring love fueled their spirits, providing the foundation upon which their dreams would eventually take shape. For in the depths of their souls, they knew that their wish to become parents would one day be fulfilled, and when that day arrived, their hearts would overflow with an immeasurable and transformative love that would forever change their lives.

Chapter 2

It was a cold November morning when Ethan sat at his usual bus stop on the corner of Olive Street, engrossed in a spy novel while enjoying the melodies of The Doobie Brothers through his wireless earbuds.

A frail, silver haired elderly man in what appeared to be his pajamas approached Ethan waving for his attention.

Ethan turned down the volume on his earbuds, his curiosity piqued.

"Sorry, I didn't quite catch what you said," Ethan responded politely, trying to be attentive despite his confusion.

"Ethan, I know this is all going to sound preposterous," the elderly man began, "but forgive my urgency as we simply don't have time."

Ethan searched his memory for any prior encounters with the man. Perhaps a customer at the bar, or a relative of one of his recent patients.

"I'm sorry, sir, have we met?"

"No, not before today, but I know more about you

than you do yourself," the man replied, urgency lacing his words.

"I need you to hear me out, Ethan. Just listen. I'm uncertain how long I have, please."

The old man leaned in closer, his eyes filled with urgency and concern.

"You must understand, Ethan, our days are numbered. Time is slipping away, and soon everything you hold dear, everything you know and love in this world, will be gone."

Ethan's concern for the man's mental well-being grew. However, he chose to be patient and respectful, aware that the man might need human connection and engagement more than anything else.

The old man continued with conviction, "I've seen all our futures and it's not a world..."

Ethan discreetly turned the music up on his headphones until he couldn't hear the stranger any longer and checked the time, then felt relief when he saw the approaching bus.

With a quick glance back at the man, he made a mental note to contact his friend, Marcus, a police officer who could provide the necessary assistance, and swiftly boarded the bus.

After taking a seat, Ethan pulled his phone out of his pocket, paused the track he was listening to, and dialed Marcus' number.

"Hey, Marcus, do me a favor and send someone out to pick up an elderly man on the stop close to Olive Street. He's out of his mind and clearly off his medication. I don't believe that he would be a threat to anyone, perhaps a disturbance to the peace if left unsupervised."

Marcus, ever reliable, responded, "Ethan, no worries, I'll head out myself. It's been, let's just say, a quiet morning and I could do with a reason to get my steps in."

Ethan expressed his gratitude. "Thank you, my friend. He's just lost, in both senses of the word."

Curiosity getting the best of him, Marcus asked, "How crazy are we talking?"

"You know I don't like that talk, Marcus. Everyone deserves respect. I'm just concerned for his well-being and potentially causing upset to others," Ethan responded.

"Understood. You got it! Did he say much to you?" Marcus asked.

"Nothing that made any sense," Ethan replied, a touch of empathy in his voice. "Thanks again. Beers tonight? First ones on me."

"First two - it's Friday, my man, nowhere to be tomorrow," Marcus replied with a chuckle.

"You got it, thanks," Ethan said, ending the call.

He returned to his book, restarting the track he had paused earlier. Deep down, he knew that reaching out to Marcus would come at a cost, likely a favor to be cashed in later, but the wellbeing of the elderly man was worth it.

Resolving to finish his shift on time, and to limit his alcohol intake afterward, Ethan hoped to spend a few precious hours with Nicole. He cherished their time together and knew that nurturing their relationship was just as important as the responsibilities he had taken on.

Chapter 3

That day, Ethan wrapped up his shift at the Silver Street Practice ahead of schedule and made his way to the bar for his evening work.

Situated on Main Street, directly across from the Greenfield Public Library and the Fire Department, The Ink & Ember held a special place in the community. It was founded by three generations of firefighter families, who had a deep connection to the town. The bar's strategic location made it a favorite among students of all ages, providing a casual gathering spot, while also serving as the go-to place for service men and women in Greenfield.

The walls of The Ink & Ember were decorated with framed pictures of firefighting teams and articles dating back 60 years, showcasing the rich history and legacy of the local fire department.

When Ethan's boss, Keith, took over the bar, he introduced some changes to enhance the experience for the patrons.

One corner of the bar was extended to create a small library area, where people could enjoy a drink while indulging in their favorite books.

This innovation attracted older students from the nearby library, offering them a more relaxed and laid-back environment compared to the traditional library setting.

However, as the evening approached, The Ink & Ember transformed its ambiance to cater to the hardworking families of Greenfield. The main lights were dimmed, allowing the nostalgic neon signs to illuminate the space, creating an intimate and inviting atmosphere. The music was turned up, filling the air with a lively energy that encouraged people to unwind and enjoy their time in the bar.

At around 9 pm, Marcus arrived and took a seat at the bar.

Marcus Davis was a man who effortlessly commanded respect with his authoritative presence and embodied an attractive dynamic that unfolded as the clock struck 9pm. Beyond his role as a seasoned police officer, he embraced an easy-going nature that reminded him of the importance of valuing each passing moment. Despite his age of forty-seven, his sturdy and well-built physique defied expectations. Relaxed and laid-back, he could be found most evenings, sitting at the bar, dressed casually in vibrant Hawaiian shirts. His charming presence carried a subtle tribute to his Caribbean roots, revealed through the refined tones of his warm complexion and the reverberations of resettlement in his cultural expressions.

"Good evening, my friend. I'll have a reset, please. It's been quite a day," he greeted Ethan.

Understanding what his friend meant, Ethan poured a whiskey on the rocks and placed it in front of Marcus. "This one's on me. My shift ends at 10. Let's catch up then," Ethan suggested.

Marcus raised his glass in gratitude, nodding his agreement.

Ethan returned to serve other customers, but as he started to pour, the pump splattered and choked. "Barrel change, I'll sort it," Ethan called out to his staff before heading down into the cellar to resolve the issue.

Upon his return upstairs, heart-breaking melodies filled the air.

Ethan, turning to his colleague, Cindy asked "What is this, "America?" Referring to the music playing on the jukebox.

"Marcus, he likes to set a tone, what can I say?" Cindy replied, closing the register.

Ethan remarked, "Well, he has certainly set one."

On completion of his drinks order. Ethan walked over to where Marcus was sitting. "I like America, as much as the next guy but" Don't Cry Baby," on a Friday night, in a bar, what are you going for here?"

"I'm a sensitive soul, Ethan." Marcus replied with a hint of mischief in his voice.

"You got that right. Any other sad songs on tonight's playlist?" Ethan replied.

"Troubled souls drink more, my friend. I'm just a silent salesman, so you should be grateful," Marcus playfully remarked.

This was an ongoing joke that Marcus liked to pull whenever Ethan was working. And by now all the staff had embraced it.

After Ethan's shift, Marcus convinced him to stay for a drink.

"You know, I couldn't find a trace of that old boy anywhere. I drove around for an hour, exploring all the back streets, but he seemed to have disappeared. Probably someone who had lost him picked him up again."

"Yeah, that's probably what happened, " Ethan agreed. "By the way, what happened to getting your steps in?"

Marcus chuckled. "Well, I walked here, and I'll be walking home. That should be enough steps for the day, don't you think?"

Ethan clinked his bottle against Marcus' and took a last sip before placing it on the bar, adding it to the other empties that Cindy was collecting.

"Trying to do my job too?" Cindy jokingly remarked. She was a curly-haired blonde in her fifties, who had been working at the bar for over thirty years and had no desire to leave the town or the county she loved.

"Your shift is over, Ethan. Go home to your beautiful wife!" Cindy chided him with a warm smile.

"On my way out, Cindy. Is Peter meeting you here at closing time?" Ethan asked.

"He sure is, honey. Now you go on and get out of here!" Cindy replied.

Ethan glanced over and saw that Marcus was already engaged in one of his cop stories with Patricia, a free-spirited student who worked the late shift after Ethan left for the day. "You two have a good night, and no shots for Marcus" he called out.

Marcus turned to Ethan with a mischievous grin. "No shots? Where's your sense of adventure, Ethan? Sure, see you soon, buddy."

Ethan bid farewell to his friends and made his way back home, arriving a little later than he had hoped. He slipped into bed next to Nicole, who had drifted off to sleep while watching a show on her iPad.

Chapter 4

With the arrival of the weekend, Ethan toiled away tending to the vibrant blooms and trimming the lush greenery in the front garden. As he immersed himself in his gardening tasks, an animated elderly lady, whom he assumed to be in her late eighties, approached him.

Having witnessed the devastating effects of dementia on his wife's grandparents and her decline in health, he couldn't help but feel a jolt of shock at the sight of this woman's apparent vitality.

"Have you given any more thought to what I told you yesterday, Ethan?" the lady inquired, her voice carrying an air of urgency.

Perplexed, Ethan stammered, "Excuse me? I'm sorry, but I'm not sure I understand."

Her gaze fixed on him, the elderly lady continued, "I apologize for the confusion, Ethan. I know how bewildering this all must sound. But time is running out, and I must know if you are willing to lend your help."

Words escaped Ethan, his hands outstretched in a gesture of bewilderment, searching for meaning.

Undeterred, the elderly lady pressed on, her voice intent on conveying importance, "You see, Ethan, when you've traversed time as many times as I have, moving from one host to another becomes almost as mundane as catching a bus. But now, if we are to save everything you see before you, and the very fabric of this world, I need you to bear the weight of the information I'm about to share with you."

Setting aside a bag of soil and removing his gardening gloves, Ethan motioned for her to join him on the small bench outside their home.

"Please, have a seat. Am I dreaming? Is any of this real?" he questioned, his mind teetering on the edge of disbelief.

With a solemn expression, the elderly lady replied, "No, I'm afraid this is all too real."

Aware of the overwhelming magnitude of what she was about to divulge, she continued. "I understand that it's a lot to process, and your instinct may be to call your police officer friend, Marcus. But trust me when I say that even Marcus won't be able to aid us. No one on this earth can stop what is coming next."

Chapter 5

In both encounters, Ethan had found himself face-to-face with the same person, or rather, the same consciousness. They referred to themselves as "transients" and claimed to be time travelers from the future, specifically from a project known as "The Yesterday Exchange."

The woman had divulged personal and intimate information from Ethan's past, revealing the hidden moments when he had sought refuge in the depths of the woods, seeking safety and comfort from the wrath of his foster father. Those were the times when his foster father's frustrations, stemming from a challenging day at work or an evening drowned in alcohol, would erupt into violence. The details shared were so intimate and deeply rooted in Ethan's memories that it left him astonished, realizing that this stranger possessed knowledge that was known only to him, locked away from the prying eyes of the world.

Her voice carried a compassionate tone as she spoke, her words tinged with empathy and concern. "There was a devastating event on October 5th, 2027, in the Pioneer Valley. It caused a disruption in atmospheric molecules, resulting in a rapid depletion of oxygen.

Within just a few hours, three-quarters of all life perished due to asphyxiation."

"In the aftermath," she continued, "survivors discovered a breakthrough. They found a way to transfer consciousness and memories from the future to individuals in the past. However, only those with strong mental resilience were deemed suitable for transference. It was a challenging process, fraught with early failures and fatal consequences. The younger generations often rejected the transfer, and if a transient stayed within a host for too long, they risked losing their own memories and becoming absorbed into the host's identity."

Her expression softened, a touch of seriousness in her tone. "We also established The Waypoint, a base in the past which served as a sort of 'saved game,' if you like—a bubble in the past, staffed by younger hosts replicating future technology."

"On these occasions our travelers took over the host of much younger subjects, those who have had little influence and have been forgotten by society. They serve as hosts for longer-term transients, assigned to gather vital intelligence while remaining isolated. If the transient stays too long, they may lose their own memories and become intertwined with the host's identity, potentially losing themselves in the process."

Ethan's mind grappled with the gravity of the

situation. "That's unimaginable!"

"To transmit gathered information to the future, "she explained, "a unique method was employed. The knowledge was leapfrogged across time, utilizing safe deposit boxes stored in the longest surviving bank in Massachusetts. These boxes were strategically placed at the closest possible point in time before the catastrophic event occurred. Transients were assigned to monitor and safeguard these deposit boxes, ensuring the safe transfer of information."

She paused, her gaze reflective. "The Waypoint team initially started with ten carefully chosen strong and brilliant minds. But now, only two of them remain. If the timeline could be altered for the better," she said, her voice filled with hope, "eliminating the need for The Yesterday Exchange and ensuring no threat to civilization as it was known, those two remaining transients could be left behind."

"Of course," she acknowledged, "the whole situation posed a potential paradox. But technically, the technology would still exist in 2025, allowing the remaining transients to make any necessary final preparations before their own existence was inevitably erased by the host's consciousness."

Her tone shifted, growing urgent once more. "This is where it gets interesting, Ethan. We discovered recently that two years prior to our doomsday, there was an isolated incident that had not been properly accounted for. It occurred on a small commuter night bus, here in Greenfield. Everyone on board, except for a single man, lost their lives."

"The townsfolk attributed the deaths to a leak of engine fumes, as the victims appeared to have suffocated."

She continued in a composed tone, "The lone survivor, John Miller, emerged from a broken home, burdened by the tragic loss of his older brother, Michael, during a mall shooting in 1988 and the weight of his father's passing soon after. However, the pieces of Miller's life puzzle don't fit neatly together. He lived as a lonely working-class man, toiling away in underpaid farming jobs, seemingly disconnected from any special projects or scientific endeavors. Without any guiding influences and consumed by grief and despair from an early age, our assumption is that these traumatic events propelled this seemingly ordinary man down a dark path, eventually entangling him in dangerous terrorist activities."

"There is one more crucial piece of information I need to share with you, Ethan," the transient said solemnly, her voice tinged with empathy.

Ethan, already wide-eyed from the overwhelming flood of details dropped on him, was pushed beyond his limits.

"You see, Ethan, on the day of the initial incident, two days from now, you were among the deceased."

The weight of this revelation crushed him, leaving him paralyzed with shock. He attempted to rise, only to collapse to the ground in a crumpled heap. Summoning his last bit of strength, he knelt with his hands supporting his trembling body, overwhelmed by a wave of emotions.

With every passing moment and word spoken the lady appeared to stumble as if fighting the cold calling of death itself.

Taking a moment to compose herself, she drew a deep breath and continued, her voice filled with a mix of determination and empathy. "We want to send your consciousness back to the host of John Miller's older brother on the day of the shooting. Our goal is to delve into the Miller family's story, acknowledging that the loss of his brother and father served as catalysts, setting off a chain of events. However, there may be deeper layers yet to uncover, shedding light on the path of destruction he embarked upon."

Ethan, still incredulous, managed to pull himself up. The tale unfolding before him seemed like something out of a science fiction novel.

"And what about Nicole, her family, my friends in

Franklin County," Ethan asked, his voice filled with concern and desperation. "Did any make it?"

Tingling with desperation and a sense of urgency, she answered: "Only a handful of people in this state survived, none of whom I can confirm by name."

It was an outrageous story, and Ethan adamantly refused to accept that following the weekend, he would be dead, along with his wife, loved ones, and most of humanity just two years later.

"We cannot force you to undertake this mission, Ethan," she emphasized, her tone filled with understanding. "It must be your decision. We possess the technology, located at a Waypoint station in this time, to extract you at the moment of death and send you back to 1988."

"Ethan, my time in this host is running out. I need an answer." As disbelief coursed through Ethan, he mustered the strength to stand. With the transient's time fading, she pressed for a decision. Ethan nodded, and she peacefully passed away beside him.

Chapter 6

The survivors of the catastrophic event on October 5th, 2027, found themselves in a world where working was no longer a necessity and, with an abundance of food from the remaining farms, life should have been paradise. However, the truth was far from idyllic. The once thriving, now sparse population found themselves permeated with an overwhelming sense of loneliness.

Whether it was a lingering effect of the event or simply a loss of purpose, people were losing their will to carry on. The birth rate plummeted, signaling the impending end of humanity.

The event's impact wasn't limited to humans alone; it had devastating consequences for all land-based life. Species like rare birds, sea lions in the Pacific, red pandas native to the eastern Himalayas and southwestern China, rhinoceroses, and elephants found in Africa, and Southeast Asia were among species now extinct, forever lost to the world.

Yet, amidst the desolation, the seas thrived. With the absence of overfishing and pollution, marine life flourished. It was a bittersweet sight, a reminder of what the world had lost on land.

As the years passed, the younger generation, the last to survive, witnessed the gradual decay of their once vibrant cities. Bustling metropolises now lay in silent ruins, a mere shell of their former glory. Buildings crumbled under the weight of time, as nature relentlessly reclaimed what was once its own. Vines snaked their way through streets and sidewalks, while grass blanketed the remnants of human civilization.

The survivors faced a somber truth: time was not their ally. With each passing day, the world slipped further into a desolate state, the remnants of humanity struggling to find purpose and hope in a world that seemed determined to erase their existence.

In this new world of abundance and freedom from mundane jobs, the future still held some promise for humanity.

A group of surviving scientists, hailing from the prestigious M.I.T in Cambridge, Massachusetts, focused their efforts on a ground-breaking technology. Their goal was to capture the essence of a person, storing their consciousness and memories as a safeguard against any catastrophic events that could wipe out the human species. This ambitious endeavor aimed to preserve the collective knowledge of humanity for future generations or even for the exploration of other worlds.

After two decades of dedicated research, the scientists made a significant breakthrough.

They successfully extracted the electrochemical charges responsible for thought and memory from the human brain. However, the excitement waned as scientists struggled to find a functional prototype capable of containing the sophisticated complexity of the human mind. No artificial creation could replace the intricate workings of the organic brain.

Meanwhile, surviving engineers at NASA explored alternatives to faster-than-light space travel. They recognized the challenges of traversing vast distances across both time and space. Even if interstellar travel was achieved, returning to the world left behind would mean arriving in a future drastically different from the one they'd left. It would be a selfish pursuit, as everyone and their descendants would be long gone upon the traveler's return.

Yet, within the realm of scientific exploration, another avenue presented itself at NASA. The study of light using waves to transfer data, instead of a physical form.

It was at this intersection of scientific pursuits that the minds behind all the projects converged. By combining the extraction of consciousness with directional light speed data wave technology, a remarkable possibility emerged for the transference of minds across great distances in time and space.

Leading the charge was the brilliant scientist, Geoffrey Teller. Teller was afflicted by Alzheimer's disease, and its rapid progression threatened to rob him of his intellect. However, older members of the scientific community selflessly stepped forward, volunteering as hosts for the first transfers. They sacrificed their remaining years of life in pursuit of scientific advancement and the preservation of knowledge.

With this pivotal transfer, The Yesterday Exchange was born, setting the stage for a remarkable journey that would bridge the realms of science, consciousness, and time itself.

They possessed the ability to travel, but what they lacked was a guiding map to navigate through time. It took a decade for that possibility to emerge. As the population rapidly dwindled, the race to safeguard humanity was intensifying, with time running out.

Chapter 7

David Carter, The Yesterday Exchange's most seasoned time traveler, had returned from his latest jump to communicate with Ethan in 2025. After surviving a close call in a host from his recent journey and passing the thorough checks by the "arrivals" team at M.I.T, he was discharged.

Having changed from his all-in-one suit back into civilian clothing, he walked across the crumbling remnants of the once-thriving city of Cambridge towards the on-site food station, surrounded by tall infrastructure now intertwined with nature's reclamation. David settled on a bench with a salad and a cup of black coffee.

Kaya Redfox, another of the Exchange's researchers and a friend approached David from across the plaza. With tall stature and wavy brown hair, Kaya Redfox carried herself with a quiet confidence, her spirit reflecting her rich Native American heritage.

Kaya called out to him, "So, how was your trip, David? Did he take the deal?"

David took a moment, savoring a sip of his coffee before responding.

"You know, it's a hard pill to swallow, being told you're going to die in a couple of days. But it sunk in on my second attempt."

Kaya's concern was evident as she mentioned the tense moments during David's journey. "It was getting tight there for a few moments. We didn't know if we'd get you back. That host was unstable."

David chuckled sarcastically, his voice carrying a tinge of dark humor. "Unstable is an understatement, Kaya. I was practically wearing a corpse!"

Kaya shot him a frown, then shifted the conversation to the next stage of the plan.

"So, are we sending orders back to The Waypoint in 25'? Get them ready for the connection?"

David's exhaustion was palpable as he replied. "He doesn't have much of a choice. He's dead if he stays. Send someone back with the details."

Kaya raised an eyebrow, considering the alternative. "You don't want to deliver it yourself?"

A note of exasperation crept into David's voice. "Are you kidding me? Two jumps in two days, both to high-risk hosts? I'm shattered!"

Kaya nodded disdainfully. "Ok, David, we'll send Jackson back. He hasn't had much action recently.

Fingers crossed this is the last transfer any of us have to make in our timeline."

David's tone turned somber as he contemplated the possible outcomes. "If this all goes to plan, you and I will cease to exist."

The conversation hung in the air, a weighty reminder of the immense stakes and sacrifices that were the price of their work.

Chapter 8

At the Turner household that evening, an air of stillness hung heavy in the atmosphere. Caught between familiar reality and the impending unknown, Ethan chose his words carefully.

He explained how he had encountered an elderly lady seemingly lost and disoriented and had extended an invitation for her to sit with him, hoping to gather information to contact her caregiver.

The coroner, who was familiar with the family, contacted the deceased's daughter Miss. Peterson, who had been at home with her mother that day.

As the daughter arrived on the scene, witnessing her mother being lifted into the vehicle, she opened the body bag and gently kissed her mother on the forehead, bidding her a final farewell.

In conversation with the police, the daughter revealed that her mother had been bedridden for several months, too weak to even lift her head, let alone venture two streets away.

Hoping that a small white lie would bring some comfort, Ethan interjected, saying, "I'm sorry for your loss. Your mother told me she wanted to feel the breeze and walk in the sunlight." Grateful for Ethan's compassion in her mother's final moments, Miss. Peterson expressed her thanks.

By now, the sun was setting, casting a darkened tone over the surroundings. The coroner had departed, and Marcus and his team had finished their duties, taking statements from both Ethan and the neighbor, who could only provide confirmation of what she had observed from across the street.

Marcus finished packing up his patrol vehicle and approached Ethan, who sat on the porch with Nicole. 'Are you going to be, okay?' he asked with genuine concern.

Looking up at Marcus, Ethan nodded, acknowledging his support.

"In that case, we'll get packed up and give you two some space," Marcus said, understanding the weight of the situation. 'There was nothing you could have done, Ethan. Mrs. Peterson's time had come, and she found peace in passing somewhere safe, in the company of kind-hearted individuals like yourself."

"Thank you, Marcus," Ethan replied, gratitude evident in his eyes as he glanced at his friend.

"Take care, you two," Marcus bid them farewell, making his way back to his car, leaving Ethan and Nicole to confront their emotions in the stillness of the evening.

In the house, Nicole prepared tea for them both while Ethan sat silently in his chair. Sensing his need for reassurance, she approached him and gently placed her hand on his shoulder. "Put something on, baby," she whispered, her voice filled with warmth and understanding.

Ethan understood exactly what she was doing. There was a profound comfort in the ritual of playing music, a way to escape the weight of the day. As he flipped through his record collection, he noticed that his copy of Rumours by Fleetwood Mac, was in the wrong place. He smiled, knowing it was Nicole's doing. "That one will do," she called out, her voice filled with affection.

Meeting her gaze, Ethan's heart swelled with love for his wife. "Of course, my love," he replied, his voice filled with tenderness. Carefully, he removed the vinyl from its sleeve and placed it on the turntable. As the needle gently touched the grooves, the familiar melodies of "Second-hand News" filled the room, instantly infusing their home with an uplifting energy, the power of music transporting them to a place where worries seemed distant.

Nicole returned to the living space, setting Ethan's tea on the table beside his chair, before settling on the couch, engrossed in news stories on her phone. Meanwhile, Ethan relaxed in his chair, allowing the music to wash over him, replacing the heaviness of the day with its harmonies.

But in that moment, surrounded by the melodies and rhythms, Ethan realized the preciousness of his time with Nicole. If these were to be their final moments together, he vowed not to waste them. Rising from his chair, he walked over to her and gently reached out to take her hand. Looking up at him, she met his gaze, her eyes filled with love, intertwining their fingers. "Could I have this dance?" Ethan asked.

A smile bloomed on her lips as she rose to her feet, pulling him close. In sync with the music, they swayed together, moving seamlessly from room to room.

Their surroundings faded into the background as their focus became solely each other.

With each step, their connection deepened, their love transcending the boundaries of time and space.

"I love you, Baby," Ethan whispered, his voice filled with affection. Nicole returned a whisper "You are a good man, and I'm grateful that lady found you today."

As the record played on, crackling softly, the final song on the first side began—the melodic piano of 'Songbird.' Nicole nestled her head against Ethan's chest, swaying in perfect harmony with him. This was her favorite song on the album, and it had been playing in the restaurant on their second date, the night she realized he was the one.

As the last notes of the song faded, Ethan broke the silence, contemplating whether to flip the record to the other side. Slowly, Nicole shook her head, her eyes filled with tenderness. Still holding his hand, she led him upstairs to their bedroom, their connection unbreakable.

Chapter 9

The following morning, Ethan woke as the sun rose, light creeping through the shutters of their bedroom window.

It was too early to get up or wake Nicole, so he nestled into her as she slept. He felt the warmth transfer from her body to his, his slightly cooler against her radiant heat. Nicole's internal engine always ran a few degrees hotter than his own.

His mind began to drift, conjuring vivid images of a future they both yearned for. Playing with a child in the sandpit at the local park. Strolling together, their arms extended to cradle the tiny being.

But as his daydream drifted into deeper territory, a shadow cast itself over his mind. A haunting image emerged, a recurring theme from his past—the woman who had given him life yet abandoned him.

Questions surged through his mind, accompanied by a pang of sadness and confusion. Why had she left him behind? Did she sense something was wrong, a flaw in him that she couldn't bear? The queries lingered unanswered.

Just as the weight of these thoughts threatened to consume him, his daydream was broken, Nicole stirred, emitting a soft, sleepy moan. Her body instinctively sought comfort within his embrace, attempting to stretch and find her own sense of serenity.

The clock on the bedside table ticked closer to 6:30 am, the room flooding with morning sunlight, casting a warm glow upon their entwined figures.

Ethan's mind filled with a mix of emotions, contemplating the limited time he had left with his beloved if the revelations of the past 24 hours were indeed true.

The overwhelming urge to be by Nicole's side intensified, his desire to cherish every moment with her consuming his thoughts. It was a Sunday, a day meant for being together, and he had no intention of leaving her side, not even for a moment.

He closed his eyes once more, nuzzling his face against Nicole's shoulder, their bodies fitting together perfectly. In the embrace of her warmth and the rhythm of her breath, he found balance, drifting back into a peaceful slumber.

Chapter 10

After what felt like the longest day of Ethan's life, he questioned every second and replayed all the events of the last two days. It was Monday evening, and he had finished working at his practice, feeling mentally and physically exhausted. He gathered the paperwork from his recent clients, meticulously organizing and filing them. Leaving his colleagues who were still in a session to lockup, he left the building and headed to the bus stop across the street.

Ethan was unable to shake off the chilling sensation that gripped him.

Having boarded the bus at Silver Street and taken a seat by the window, Ethan took a deep breath, and closed his eyes, desperately trying to shield his thoughts from the impending scene. The knowledge of his imminent death lingered in his mind, casting an ominous cloud of anticipation.

The atmosphere inside the bus suddenly grew oppressive, as if a sinister presence lurked in the air. The temperature soared, suffocating the passengers, as if the air conditioner had transformed into a malevolent force working against them.

Beads of sweat formed on Ethan's forehead, his palms moistening with a mix of anxiety and fear. A wave of unease swept through the bus, each passenger grappling with their own invisible torment.

Desperate for reassurance, Ethan reached out, seeking relief in the company of others. But to his dismay, he found them all caught in the same clutches of agony, their faces contorted in pain. Panic surged through his veins, rendering him dizzy and disoriented. Through blurred vision, he caught sight of one man, seemingly untouched by the heat and stifling presence, his gaze fixed on Ethan with an eerie detachment.

Time seemed to freeze for a fleeting moment, as if the universe held its breath in anticipation. Then, in an instant, the bus screeched to a violent halt, crashing into a row of parked cars. The deafening collision shattered the air, leaving behind a haunting silence.

In the aftermath, as dust settled and the wreckage lay strewn about, an eerie stillness prevailed. The bus transformed into a vessel of silence, a tomb of shattered dreams and unanswered questions.

Chapter 11

A fraction of a second after his final breath, Ethan experienced a disorienting sensation as if his very being had been violently ripped away, accompanied by a throbbing headache, and a symphony of muffled sounds. As Ethan's senses gradually sharpened, he realized he was no longer on the bus. Instead, chaos engulfed the scene as gunshots pierced the air, causing panic-stricken crowds to scatter in all directions. The neon signs of the illuminated stores flickered and blurred in his vision, adding to the disorientation.

Amidst the overwhelming sensory overload, Ethan's attention zeroed in on the anguished cries of a young boy. He caught the child's look of sheer terror, hands pressed tightly against his ears, and a face contorted with fear. He screamed, looking directly at him, "Mike!" Assuming him to be the younger brother of Michael the transient had described, Ethan struggled to comprehend the weight of responsibility that now rested upon this seemingly insignificant boy.

In his innocence and vulnerability, he represented the hopes and dreams of countless lives. "This was the man to end everything?" Ethan whispered to himself, his voice barely audible over the commotion.

Extending a reassuring hand, Ethan mustered a calm and steady voice, attempting to offer comfort to the trembling child. "Don't worry, we'll make it through this. Just stay close to me." Together, they maneuvered through the mall, seeking cover from the indiscriminate gunfire that shattered glass and caused chaos around them.

Taking cover behind a trash can, they watched as the gunman emerged on the stairs, approaching their location. A girl, injured and in pain, huddled beside them, her shoulder grazed by a stray bullet. With a determined gaze, Ethan locked eyes with their newfound companion, silently conveying his plan through a shared understanding.

Addressing the tearful girl, he spoke with urgency. "Are you with us?" Her nod, filled with both fear and desperate hope, sealed their alliance. "On the count of three, we make a run for safety," Ethan declared, gripping the young boy's hand tightly.

"One... Two... Three... Go!" With synchronized movements, the trio weaved through the frantic crowd of shoppers, their collective survival instinct guiding their every step. As they approached the protective presence of the Greenfield Police, Paramedics swarmed the area, attending to the wounded, while one officer, clad in a bulletproof vest, swiftly intervened to shield them from harm.

Guiding them to a place of relative safety.

Inside the mall, the gunshots continued, reverberating through the halls. Panic and fear consumed the atmosphere. Amidst the chaos, a police radio crackled nearby, broadcasting a man's voice, "10-68, he's down, repeat 10-68!"

Ethan, now occupying Michael's consciousness, understood the weight of his mission. Just as the transient had warned, he had stepped into Michael's life, altering the course of events, and replacing his existence. The responsibility he bore was immense, and the emotional toll weighed heavily upon him. But for now, his focus remained on the young boy as the journey had just begun, with the uncertainties of the future looming ahead.

Chapter 12

Following the thorough medical examination at Baystate Franklin Medical Centre, the dedicated hospital staff diligently tended to the Miller boys' minor bumps and grazes, remnants of their harrowing experience at the Greenfield shopping mall.

Dr. Torres, the attending physician, approached Janeane Miller with a caring smile. "Mrs. Miller, we have taken care of their physical injuries, and they should heal well. However, I want to emphasize the importance of monitoring their emotional well-being in the days to come. It might be beneficial to consider counseling services to help them process what they went through."

Relief etched on her face, Mrs. Miller embraced her sons tightly, feeling their warmth and reassuring presence. She whispered in their ears, "You both did so well today. I love you more than words can express."

Mr. Michael Miller Senior, standing tall beside his family, gently placed his hand on the heads of his sons, a gesture of love and protection. His voice trembled slightly as he spoke, his emotions unmistakable.

"I'm incredibly proud of you, Michael. You showed tremendous courage in the face of danger. Our family is stronger because of you."

Ethan, still grappling with the unfamiliarity of this time and the trauma of the mall incident, and inhabiting a different body, walked alongside the Miller family.

Despite his inner turmoil, he made a genuine effort to blend in and be present in this intimate moment. Deep down, he understood the importance of family support and solidarity during times of adversity.

The family embarked on their journey home from the hospital, united and ready to face the challenges that lay ahead, oblivious to the stranger that walked beside them.

Chapter 13

After a short journey, as the car turned onto Cleveland Street, the Miller family's home came into view, surrounded by neatly lined houses and leafy trees that shaded the sidewalks, creating a sense of peace.

Pulling into the driveway, the car came to a gentle halt. The residence, a two-story house with a white exterior. Flowerbeds adorned the front yard, showcasing an array of colorful blossoms that swayed in the gentle breeze.

Mr. Miller turned off the engine, and the family stepped out of the car, greeted by the familiar scent of fresh cut grass and blooming flowers, along with the distant sound of a baseball game in the nearby athletics field.

As the family entered, Ethan took a moment to survey his surroundings. The home exuded a cozy and welcoming atmosphere. The entryway featured a patterned wallpaper that added a touch of charm. The polished hardwood flooring, a labor of love for Michael Miller Senior, added warmth to the space.

The living room beckoned as a comfortable gathering spot, decorated with Mrs. Miller's handmade curtains gracing the large windows, and featuring a well-loved sofa, armchair, and entertainment center.

The kitchen boasted practical laminate countertops, enhanced by robust wooden cabinetry and appliances reminiscent of the time.

The large sliding glass doors provided a glimpse of the backyard, filling the space with natural light. As Ethan made his way upstairs, he discovered the parents' room, a shared family bathroom, and the children's bedrooms.

"You alright, honey?" Janeane called up the stairs to her son.

Ethan, looking down into the hallway, replied, "Yes, just a little disoriented, is all."

"To be expected, my love. Do you need anything to eat? A soda?" Janeane asked, her concern evident.

Ethan, wanting some time alone, threw a smile her way and responded, "I'm OK... Mom. I just need some time."

"Call down if you change your mind," Janeane offered before turning to leave.

"Thanks, I will," Ethan replied softly before making his way into John's bedroom.

The room was filled with vibrant posters proudly displaying John's passion for movies such as The Goonies and Teen Wolf, alongside magazine cut-outs featuring his music idols, Van Halen and Def Leppard. The walls were adorned with photos capturing the summer adventures of Michael and John.

The brothers had previously shared this space, until Michael had requested more privacy in his senior year. This fitted Ethan's needs very well. Due to Michael taking the box room, the two brothers had continued to study together, despite Michael's occasional frustration from stepping on pieces of John's Lego.

Desks with scattered schoolbooks, notebooks filled with doodles and aspirations, and the occasional science project in progress. It was here that they spent countless hours immersed in their studies, supporting each other through the challenges of school.

Above the center of the room, a papier-mâché recreation of the Earth hung, displaying intricate details that traced the contours of countries and continents. Painted stars adorned the ceiling, a handcrafted effort by their father, who took great pride in adding a touch of wonder to their once shared space.

Stepping back into the hallway, Ethan entered the box room, which was noticeably tidier than John's.

It contained a small space with a single bed, bedside table, and wardrobe for clothes. Posters of baseball heroes attached to the walls, while school medals were neatly displayed on shelves. Framed snapshots of the family, including one of Michael holding a large rainbow trout alongside an Asian boy.

Exiting the room and stepping into the hallway, Ethan made his way to the family bathroom, ensuring that the door was securely locked behind him.

The reflection seemed almost like a moving photograph, a glimpse into a parallel existence.

Michael was slightly shorter than Ethan, a fresh-faced young man with tangled dark blonde hair.

Despite the mere 10-year age difference between Ethan and his host, the lines on Ethan's own face bore a distinct and profound prominence. These visible marks of time and experience were evidence of the struggles and challenges he had faced before embarking on his fresh start in Greenfield.

Ethan, gently manipulating the skin around Michael's cheeks, found himself questioning the very fabric of his existence, pondering the authenticity and reality of his current circumstances.

His time of reflection was abruptly interrupted by a call from downstairs.

"Honey?" Janeane called up the stairs.

Ethan opened the bathroom door and asked, "Yes?"

"George is on the phone. Do you want to speak to him now, or should I ask him to call back?" Janeane inquired.

"I'll speak to him later, thanks, Mom," Ethan replied, unsure of who George was but not ready to engage in conversation just yet.

After ensuring the family had gathered in the living room and the sound of the television filled the house, Ethan seized the moment to make his move. With utmost care, he descended the stairs and discreetly stepped out into the tranquil backyard. Embracing the solitude, he reached for a basketball resting on the patio, his fingers wrapping around its familiar texture.

Adjacent to the garage, a basketball hoop dangled from its position, catching Ethan's gaze. Standing there he found himself lost in contemplation rather than attempting a shot.

As waves of memories and emotions flooded his mind, thoughts of Nicole pierced his thoughts, overwhelming him with grief. Tears streamed down his face as he grappled with the weight of the day's events, seeking comfort in his own privacy.

Janeane stood at the kitchen window, her gaze fixed on her son standing on the patio, his sobs filling the air.

Recognizing his need for solitude in the aftermath of the day's events, she honored his request and gave him the space he sought.

As she wiped away her own tears, she picked up the soda she had poured for John and made her way back to the living room.

Chapter 14

The first night proved to be the most challenging for Ethan as he found it nearly impossible to find rest in his unfamiliar surroundings.

The weight of the day's extraordinary events bore heavily on his mind, but he had to maintain an appearance of normalcy.

In this foreign time, inhabiting a body that didn't belong to him and residing within a family that was not his own, he sought comfort beneath Michael's duvet. Nestled within its comforting embrace, he turned his back to the room, seeking a semblance of privacy and composure.

With closed eyes, he conjured the image of his beloved wife and clung to the memory of their final moments together, drawing strength from their love in the face of uncertainty.

Chapter 15

In those first few days following the mall shooting, Ethan had a difficult time adjusting to the fact that he was not only in the year 1988 but also inhabiting another person's body—a body 10 years younger than his own, just 18 years old.

The weight of his mission pressed upon him, reminding him that he must never let his knowledge slip up. Too much was at stake, and any deviation could alter the course of history.

As he settled into the house, he realized it had a completely different dynamic from his own upbringing. It was a place filled with warmth, love, and nourishment. Support and guidance permeated every corner, creating an atmosphere unlike anything he had experienced before.

The Transient had shared accounts of the tragedy that shattered this home—the loss of the older brother that sent the father spiraling into depression and alcoholism, eventually leading to the separation from his wife Janeane, just a year after the shooting.

The documented tragic fate of Michael Miller Senior, killed in a DUI accident the day after the divorce was filed, seemed impossible to comprehend at this moment.

The air was filled with a sense of togetherness and hope, a stark contrast to the future that awaited them if events were allowed to unfold as history dictated.

Despite the events his sons had been subjected to, Michael Miller Senior's spirit remained unbreakable, radiating strength and resilience. It was evident that nothing could dampen his love for his boys, and he made sure they knew it. He freely expressed his affection and admiration, leaving no doubt in their minds about his support.

Photographs, frozen fragments of cherished memories, upon the walls like a gallery of love. It was here, amidst the aroma of home-cooked meals, that Mrs. Miller's support enveloped her family, offering relief and encouragement.

In the evening, the family gathered around the table for a shared meal, a cherished tradition. They would discuss their day, sharing stories, laughter, and sometimes even tears, recounting the experience that day at the mall.

Mr. Miller worked long hours at the bank, but he made a conscious effort to prioritize his children's well-being.

He lived for the weekends, eagerly awaiting the chance to spend quality time with his beloved family. His dedication was palpable, and he actively participated in his children's lives, cherishing every moment he could be present.

As Ethan observed the dynamics of the family home, it became clear that any disruption or deviation from this loving environment would serve as a catalyst for an uncertain future. The events that were destined to transpire almost 40 years down the line hinged on the delicate balance and stability of their present lives.

The family's unity and the love that flowed within those walls were the cornerstones that held their shared destiny, unknowingly intertwining with the course of history.

Chapter 16

On the following Monday, against the advice of the Miller parents, Ethan made his way to Michael's school, determined to immerse himself in the role and time-period. Greenfield High School, a mere 10-minute walk from the family home, stood as a prominent educational institution in a charming suburban setting, exemplifying the growth and legacy of education in Greenfield.

The architecture of Greenfield High School seamlessly blended traditional brickwork with modern materials, offering a harmonious combination of classic appeal and contemporary functionality.

As Ethan approached the school gates, George was the first to greet Michael, his excitement noticeable. "Where's the little one, today?" he asked eagerly.

Ethan responded, "He's stayed home with Mom."

Jouji Sato, known as George to his friends, was a lively and talkative character. With his American Japanese heritage, he brought a unique perspective to the conversations he engaged in. With a slim frame and a keen eye for fashion, effortlessly blending classic and contemporary elements in his smart casual outfits. George and Michael had been inseparable since childhood, their shared adventures captured in the photographs at the house that Ethan studied carefully. From their recreations of Rambo in the woods to the proud snapshots of their fishing conquests along the river, their bond was evident.

George's admiration for Michael's actions during the recent incident couldn't be contained. "No surprise, man! I'm amazed you're back so soon. That was some 'Delta Force' action that went down, bro. You're like Chuck Norris!" he exclaimed with a mix of awe and humor.

Ethan couldn't help but chuckle at George's enthusiastic comparison. "Pretty sure Chuck Norris fought the terrorists, George, and didn't run away."

Unfazed, George laughed and said, "Bro, you were defending your family. That's so Hollywood! In fact, that's what I'm calling you from now on!"

"Hollywood?" Ethan questioned.

"Yes, my brother!" George affirmed with a grin, fully embracing the nickname.

Ethan smiled as he thought of his predicament, George would serve as a good cover during his assignment in 1988.

He knew that George's animated personality and ability to fill the space would keep others engaged, allowing him to blend in more easily.

They made their way to first period, with Ethan quietly relieved that George's outgoing nature would compensate for his own reserved demeanor, and understood that in this dynamic duo, George had more than enough to say for both of them.

The hallways were filled with rows of lockers, lively bulletin boards, and captivating student artwork, creating an immersive and visually stimulating environment.

The school prided itself on fostering creativity and self-expression, evident in the vivid and colorful displays that covered the walls. Each step Ethan took down the hallway revealed a testimony to the students' talents and the school's commitment to nurturing their individuality.

While John, Michael's younger brother, was in his first year of high school, he had chosen to stay home for the day, seeking safety with his mother to process the recent traumatic events.

Throughout the day, Michael's other friends reached out to offer their support upon hearing about the shooting incident.

Vacant seats scattered throughout the classrooms served as a reminder of those still on the path to recovery from their injuries and a poignant reflection on the lives lost tragically at the mall that day.

Unfortunately, such incidents had become all too common in America, and Ethan, armed with his knowledge from the future, couldn't help but feel a sense of despair knowing that the situation would only get worse.

As Ethan mingled with Michael's friends, he took mental notes of their names and the dynamics of their friendship group, careful not to arouse suspicion or reveal his advanced knowledge of the subjects being taught. He downplayed his familiarity with the curriculum, striving to blend in seamlessly and avoid drawing any unwanted attention.

Chapter 17

Upon arriving home from school that afternoon, Ethan encountered Janeane Miller in the hallway, awaiting his return.

Janeane Miller, a radiant mother, graced with a tall nurturing figure, emanated warmth, and love.

"How was your day, Michael? Was it good to see your friends?" she asked, her concern evident in her voice.

Ethan, fully immersed in his role as her son, responded in a manner befitting an 18-year-old. "Yeah, Mom, it was alright."

Mrs. Miller's eyes conveyed an unspoken invitation. "Remember, you can talk to me about anything. What happened at the mall was horrifying, and no one should have to go through that. Your father and I are here for you, whenever you're ready to share."

Ethan, touched by her compassion, managed a grateful smile. "Thanks, Mom."

She pressed on, in her words. "We are incredibly proud of you, Michael, for how you handled the situation and kept your brother safe."

"Thanks," Ethan replied, his voice laced with genuine emotion.

With a final declaration of love, she retreated to the kitchen to attend to the dinner.

Ethan watched her, a tear escaping his eye, knowing the painful truth that this loving woman, who cherished her children, was conversing with a mere apparition. Her real son had tragically lost his life that day in the mall at the hands of a truly wicked individual.

Chapter 18

By Friday, John had returned to school. Recognizing John's exceptional academic abilities, his parents and teachers collectively agreed that he exhibited such remarkable promise in school that they deemed it fitting for him to advance a grade, accelerating his progression, and enabling him to commence high school a year earlier than his peers.

However, his young age of thirteen set him apart from most of his classmates and his remarkable intellectual progress made him stand out.

From a discreet distance, Ethan carefully observed him, attentively watching his interactions with both peers in his own grade and older students. The social dynamics of the 1980s were notably different from Ethan's time, emphasizing strict gender roles and expectations.

Boys were encouraged to participate in sports, while girls were directed towards excelling in home economics. It was uncommon to find individuals who deviated from these societal norms, with boys and girls rarely sharing similar interests.

Ethan noticed a circle of older boys from the 10th grade who took pleasure in teasing John during recess, whether it was extorting his lunch money or mocking his clothing.

Aware of the delicate situation, Ethan maintained a cautious distance, contemplating how he could leverage his knowledge of John's experiences to provide guidance without exacerbating the situation.

Chapter 19

Together, Ethan and John, ventured into a world of baseball games, where the crack of the bat and the roar of the crowd filled their senses with an electrifying energy. Ethan's voice would ring out with encouragement as John swung for the fences, their bond growing stronger with each pitch.

Beyond the realm of sports, Ethan dedicated himself to guiding John through his school assignments, helping him navigate the intricacies of his homework. They would sit side by side, huddled over textbooks and notebooks, as Ethan patiently explained the complexities of algebra and dissected the mysteries of literature. The warmth of their shared studies created an atmosphere of learning and growth, with Ethan offering support and guidance.

Every evening, the family would gather around the dinner table, their laughter and conversation intertwining with the aroma of home-cooked meals. The clinking of silverware and the clatter of plates became the soundtrack of their togetherness, as they exchanged tales of their day, shared dreams, and aspirations, and forged deeper connections.

And on those cherished weekends, the Miller family embarked on adventures, venturing out into the community to explore the wonders of their town. They would attend local events, immersing themselves in the vibrancy of street fairs and festivals. And like a timeless tradition, Saturday nights were reserved for the cinema, where they would join the bustling crowds, eagerly settling into their seats to experience the magic of the silver screen.

It was during these cinematic excursions that Ethan felt himself caught between two worlds. As the opening credits rolled and the projector flickered to life, he sat among moviegoers whose gasps and whispers revealed a sense of wonder and anticipation.

Yet for Ethan, these films were not new discoveries but echoes of a past he had left behind. He watched with a bittersweet nostalgia, relishing in the shared experience while also bearing the weight of his knowledge from the future.

Among those moviegoers, Ethan observed the delight and astonishment that washed over their faces, witnessing the timeless classics unfold before their eyes. The magic of cinema transported them, evoking emotions and sparking imaginations, and Ethan couldn't help but marvel at the power of these stories that had captivated generations.

The Miller family's journey continued, their bond growing stronger with each passing day.

And within the heart of this familial cocoon, Ethan found himself both a participant and an observer, his presence a catalyst for a future yet to unfold.

Chapter 20

One late night, finding himself unable to sleep, Ethan tiptoed downstairs, to retrieve a glass of water from the kitchen.

As he quietly made his way past John's room, a strange sight caught his eye through the crack of the door—the spinning globe above John's bed.

Mystified, he furrowed his brow and cautiously pushed the door open fully, entering the room.

His intention was to close the window, which he assumed was the cause of the curious motion. Yet, to his surprise, the window was tightly shut.

His gaze shifted to John, who lay in his bed, feigning sleep with an unconvincing snore.

A hunch flared in Ethan's mind, a sense that there was more to John than met the eye. He couldn't shake off the feeling that something peculiar was happening.

Moving closer to John, he broke the silence. "Did you see that?" Ethan's voice was barely a whisper, filled with a mix of curiosity and apprehension.

John remained motionless, continuing his pretense of slumber. Ethan knew he couldn't be fooled. He pressed on, determined to uncover the truth.

"I know you're awake. Did you see the globe spinning?" Ethan's words hung in the air, waiting for a response.

In the dimly lit room, John turned over, his eyes meeting his brother's. A flicker of worry appeared in his face before he finally mustered the courage to reveal his secret.

"Hey, Mike," John began hesitantly, "I've been feeling... different lately. Like something has changed inside me. It's kind of hard to explain, but it's like my senses have gotten sharper, and I feel this strange connection to nature. Like, I can hear the wind whispering to me, and I can feel the touch of a breeze like never before."

Surprised by John's revelation, Ethan's mind raced to connect the dots.

"Wait, did you move the globe?" Ethan inquired, a mixture of astonishment and excitement coloring his words.

John nodded, a glimmer of pride shining in his eyes.

"So, I guess this would explain all your home runs lately?" Ethan's voice held a touch of admiration, recognizing the extraordinary potential residing within John.

In that moment, the room seemed to crackle with a sense of excitement, a shared understanding of the extraordinary journey they were about to embark on.

The revelation of John's hidden abilities opened a door to a world they had only glimpsed in their wildest dreams. They were bound by destiny that surpassed their ordinary lives, setting them on a path filled with wonder, discovery, and the unimaginable power that lay within John.

Chapter 21

Following that extraordinary night, the two brothers developed a new routine.

Under the veil of darkness, they ventured out after their parents had fallen asleep, seeking freedom in the vastness of a nearby field. The moonlit sky served as their only witness as they engaged in a game of catch, their laughter and the rhythmic sound of the ball connecting with their mitts breaking the silence of the night.

John's throw of the baseball soaring through the air, surpassing Ethan's by an entire length of the pitch. His new-found abilities seemed to awaken something within him, an untapped power that manifested itself in his athletic prowess. With each throw, he grew more confident, displaying his remarkable strength by propelling the ball deep into the distance.

Ethan couldn't help but feel a mixture of awe and apprehension. The gap between their skills and abilities was widening with each passing day. In the dark of night, John appeared to draw power from the blanket of stars shimmering above. His body glowing like a beacon through his pajamas.

Ethan, intrigued by this mystical phenomenon, couldn't help but voice his curiosity. "Can you feel anything when that happens?"

John turned to his brother, a glimmer of wonder in his eyes. "It tingles, Mike, like an electric current running through my veins."

Ethan nodded, contemplating the implications. "That's incredible, John. But we must find a way for you to control it, especially when we're out in public. We don't want to draw too much attention or raise any eyebrows."

John chuckled, a mischievous sparkle in his gaze. "Don't worry, bro. I'll do my best to keep it under control. We can't have people mistaking me for a walking Christmas tree."

Ethan grinned, appreciating the light-heartedness. "I know you will, John. You've always been resourceful and adaptable. Just remember, our little secret is something extraordinary."

John nodded solemnly, understanding the weight of their shared secret. "I won't let it go to waste, Mike."

As they continued to play catch with the baseball, Ethan couldn't help but contemplate the profound impact of inhabiting a younger host, and the swirling emotions it brought.

The transient, his guide from his own time, had

warned him about the potential consequences of prolonged stays in a host. The boundaries between Michael and himself were blurring, their identities becoming increasingly fragile. It was a haunting realization that urged him to cherish each fleeting moment and seek answers to the mysteries that lay ahead.

In the quiet moments of the night, they retrieved the ball and prepared for another throw.

Chapter 22

By mid-June, the strong family unit and the special bond between John and his brother continued to grow.

They shared a secret, known only to the two of them, which strengthened their connection even further.

Ethan, eager to help John understand his newfound abilities, tested him gently, pushing the boundaries of what he thought possible. Through these tests, Ethan aimed to teach John about the importance of discerning right from wrong, and the value of cherishing every life, regardless of one's personal feelings.

One afternoon after school, Ethan wandered into John's room, John appearing to look hopeless and lost. Ethan remarked, having known the cause of his troubles.

"How did it make you feel, when those boys teased you today?"

John, frustrated, replied "I felt angry, Mike, angry at myself for letting them push me around."

Ethan noticed John's fists clenching, and he could feel heat rising on John's body. The air seemed to grow humid, and Ethan felt a tightness in his own lungs.

With reassurance in his voice, Ethan exclaimed, "John, you're safe now!"

John looked up and relaxed his hands, the temperature that had been radiating off him starting to fade.

Ethan got up and opened a window to catch his breath before returning to John.

"You know, times like these are normal, and you can't let others rule your feelings. It's all about managing conflict, your own internal struggle."

Ethan continued, "Think of all the wars that started all over the world, all because those involved couldn't find the right words to explain how they felt. It is far easier to act in violence than it is to pick apart your thoughts. But those who are stronger have a responsibility to act differently. Whatever it is that makes you special, you must direct it in a positive way."

Ethan walked over to the cassette player and carefully inserted a mixtape they had created together. The act of curating playlists had always served as a grounding ritual for Ethan, even in his earlier years. His older foster brother had played a significant role, lending him an MP3 player, and guiding him in discovering music on the internet. In the face of the looming, oppressive shadow cast by his violent foster father, music became a sanctuary, a means to divert his attention from the dark thoughts that swirled within his own mind.

Jump by Van Halen came on, immediately bringing a smile to John's face.

John excitedly announced, "I really like this one, Mike."

Ethan carried on speaking "Music is a powerful tool to overcome almost anything you feel. At the least, it gives you the strength to stop the roller-coaster of emotions and truly identify them."

Ethan pulled out a comic that Janeane had bought him for helping with the chores in the last couple of weeks. It was a Superman comic.

"You can change the outcome of any situation with the power that comes from understanding your own mind. This is your superpower. You can have all the strength of Superman, but if you can't channel your thoughts, you're no better than Lex Luthor."

Curiously, John looked at Michael "So, I'm like Superman, Mike?"

Tapping his temple with his fingers, Ethan replied "You have the potential to be better.

Your superpowers come from here... and not from here." Holding a fist with his other hand. John looked up at his brother with a hint of pride. He smiled and nodded.

Music became a powerful tool for Ethan to guide and connect with John, recognizing its profound impact on the human spirit. Encouraging John to create mixtapes filled with his favorite songs, they embarked on a journey of musical exploration, selecting tracks that resonated deeply with his soul. Together, they delved into the world of power rock, discovering the magic of bands like REO Speedwagon, Night Ranger and Toto. John would eagerly listen to the radio, hitting the record button when the DJ announced a song he liked, and later meticulously editing the recordings with Ethan to create new cassettes, removing adverts and extraneous voices. It was an art form, carefully arranging the tracks to ensure a seamless listening experience and perfect timing.

As their bond deepened, John began to see his older brother in a new light, recognizing the wisdom that seemed to surpass his years. He eagerly embraced his brother's guidance and invaluable lessons, finding inspiration to be his best self.

During it all, Ethan found himself emotionally bonding with his adopted brother, fragments of Michael's memories overlapping his own.

It wasn't just the shared experiences or the incredible journey they were on; it was the love, warmth, and support that engulfed them within the walls of their home.

Their path altering the course of history, a transformation of their own souls, deepening their connection as brothers and shaping them into the individuals they were destined to become.

Together, they were writing a story of love, resilience, and the extraordinary power of family.

Chapter 23

After a day filled with the routine of school, Ethan braced himself for, yet another covert mission cloaked in the darkness of night.

Each passing day, John's powers grew stronger, and he had honed the art of concealing his extraordinary abilities.

The responsibility of being the mentor to this powerful individual was immense, but the known outcome should he trip and stumble off his trajectory was something Ethan knew was not an option.

Understanding that the loss of his brother in a traumatic experience and the lack of guidance of his father in the previous timeline was enough to throw him into decades of despair with fatal consequences.

The Yesterday Exchange had documented the bus incident, but Ethan wondered how many instances went unnoticed.

How many lives had John inadvertently affected in the lead-up to his world-altering event.

Ethan never believed John to be intentionally

malicious, rather, he saw him as someone struggling to control his powers and emotions, a factor that had led him to become somewhat reclusive throughout his life.

Ethan recognized that Michael's presence in the timeline couldn't be indefinite. Prolonged alterations to the fabric of reality carried inherent risks and could unleash unforeseen complications upon the environment.

Eventually, John would need to navigate his journey alone or find others whom he could trust with his secret. It fell upon Ethan's shoulders to prepare him for that inevitable eventuality.

Chapter 24

That evening, Janeane tasked her son Michael with picking up groceries from town.

As Ethan returned home, his eyes caught sight of an elderly homeless man sitting on the sidewalk, clutching a sign that read "hungry." Stirred by his own experiences with homelessness, Ethan felt a surge of empathy for those who had lost their way. Without hesitation, he dropped some spare change into the man's pot and placed an apple from the grocery bag beside him.

The man looked up, gratitude etched on his weathered face, and thanked Ethan for his kindness. Just as Ethan turned to walk away, he heard the man call out to him, but not by the name familiar to those in this time. Intrigued, he turned back to face the homeless man, who had risen from the ground and approached him.

"Ethan, it's David," he said, breaking the silence. "I never formally introduced myself before, and our last conversation was... let's just say, a little rushed."

Surprised to encounter the transient once again, Ethan extended his hand in a friendly gesture.

"It's a pleasure to see you again, in whatever form. I must admit, I feel caught in a rather challenging situation."

Shaking Ethan's hand, David nodded. "I understand. Time travel is a mind-bending experience, let alone being placed in another person's body."

Ethan reflected on his time in the Miller family, the unexpected warmth and love that he discovered. "This journey has shown me that the family John Miller comes from is far different than I had anticipated."

Curiosity brimming in his eyes, David inquired, "Has your time here provided any insights?"

Concerned not to reveal the truth about John's abilities, as this revelation could end with harm coming to him, Ethan chose his words. "I'm doing my best to guide him and offer him the stability he needs, much like his real brother would have. As for your time, has anything changed?"

David's expression turned woeful. "Sadly, no. But we hold onto the hope that your influence will make a difference."

Ethan, feeling a sense of urgency as he sensed fragments of himself slipping away, pressed on with his inquiry. "When will you extract me from this host?"

The response came with a cautious tone, "Long-term transients like yourself have typically lived lives with minimal interaction. We have never taken such a risk within the timeline."

Ethan's concern deepened as he contemplated the implications.

"Michael's existence was never intended within this timeline. Allowing him to remain here indefinitely could have unforeseen consequences, altering the course of events in unpredictable ways." David persisted.

"If we fail to achieve our mission in this timeline, we won't be able to extract you. In your own time, you are already deceased. In that case, we could potentially relocate you to a host, like this old boy here, but it would offer only a brief lifespan, I'm afraid."

Contemplating the weight of his own actions, Ethan wondered aloud, "And if I do succeed, what happens to the members of your team?"

"Our transients at The Waypoint are aware that if they lose contact with us, it means our impending doomsday has been averted. They have been given instructions to bring you back to the exact moment you departed from your timeline."

Ethan returned, "May I ask what happens to them

after that?"

A hint of sadness touched his eyes. "Regrettably, they will assimilate, become one with their hosts.

It's the sacrifice we all make for the hope of a better future."

Nodding in understanding, in response, Ethan offered "I'll do whatever it takes to make a difference."

David's voice carried a mix of gratitude and farewell. "That's all any of us can do, Ethan."

Suddenly, the man before Ethan convulsed and dropped to the ground, only to open his eyes a moment later, looking up at Ethan with a Bashful grin. "Apologies, young sir. I must have dozed off. Thank you again for the apple."

"You're welcome, " Ethan responded, turning around to head back to continue his way. The path ahead remained uncertain, but Ethan was resolved to push forward, hoping that his actions would eventually lead to a brighter outcome.

Chapter 25

As another week passed, the bond between the brothers grew stronger. But amidst the harmony, Ethan found himself battling conflicting thoughts of both Michael's and his own. He was aware of John's ability to control his powers, and he felt a responsibility to pass on his wisdom before he departed.

However, the question gnawed at him: What would happen if he were to leave his newfound family behind? If he stayed, somehow, would his presence create a paradox, altering the course of events?

And what about Nicole, the love of his life? If his previous existence never happened, what would become of their relationship? Would she still find happiness, get married, and start a family?

Ethan's heart ached as he grappled with these thoughts, torn between the overflowing emotions of Nicole's memories and the deepening connection to this time and place.

The choice ahead of him was a difficult one, as he weighed the potential consequences and the impact it would have on those he cared for.

That night under the cloak of darkness, John and Ethan stealthily ventured out, quietly retrieving their BMX bikes from the backyard. Their path led them across Lincoln Street, treading softly as they made their way towards the secluded woods by the Connecticut River. Hidden within the thick foliage of leafy trees, the sanctuary provided the perfect haven for their concealed activities, shielded from prying eyes and devoid of any nearby residences.

Navigating the challenging terrain, where every step required resilience and focus, they were grateful for the guiding presence of their own human torch, emanating from John, casting light through the darkness.

Upon reaching the banks of the river, a sense of calmness surrounded them. The moon's reflection danced upon the water's surface, casting a shimmering path of light toward the uninhabited Rawson Island. The gentle rustling of the river and the distant chirping of crickets echoed through the night.

Sitting on the riverbank, their bicycles parked beside them, John broke the silence with a question that weighed heavily on his mind.

"Why am I different, Mike?" he asked, his voice filled with curiosity and a touch of uncertainty.

Ethan gazed at him, his eyes reflecting a mixture of

understanding and compassion, fully attuned to John's need for reassurance. "None of us are the same, John," he began, his voice carrying a reassuring tone. "There is no template for how a person should be or what it is that makes us stand out as individuals. We are all uniquely shaped by our experiences and challenges. Throughout life, we will inevitably encounter obstacles. How we tackle these is entirely based on learning."

"But how am I different from you, Mom, and Dad?" John inquired, seeking a clearer understanding of his own identity.

Ethan's response was filled with conviction, as he recognized the significance of John's powers. "The short answer is, for whatever reason, you are special, John," Ethan explained. "Knowing that your power exists, there is a very strong possibility that others out there possess the same qualities. The mind is a powerful thing, and we have yet to unlock its full potential. My guess is that you have that ability. It explains why you are as smart as you are, your ability to move matter with your thoughts. Evolution is inevitable, and perhaps one day, all of humanity will share these traits. You are just the first to unlock these extraordinary gifts."

John's face lit up with a new-found sense of acceptance. The notion that his powers were not a flaw, but a natural progression ignited a spark of hope within him. He contemplated the possibility of others like him, wondering if he could somehow sense their presence.

Ethan's words resonated deeply with John, filling him with a sense of purpose. "So, shall we get started?" Ethan proposed, breaking the momentary silence. "We need to head back before it's too late. We don't want a repeat of the other night."

Chuckling, John replied, "Yeah, Mom wasn't too thrilled about me falling asleep in class."

"Agreed," Ethan affirmed.

"You want to try and walk on water? That could be fun," Ethan suggested playfully.

Laughing back at his brother, John responded, "Very funny, Mike. I don't think so."

"Well, we don't want to boil the fish alive, so let's keep our tests land-based," Ethan proposed, considering the potential consequences of their actions.

Grabbing a nearby rock, Ethan tossed it to John, encouraging him to throw it skyward. "Try not to hit the moon. NASA might notice a new crater," he quipped, a playful grin adorning his face.

"You think I could reach the moon?" John pondered aloud.

"I think in time, anything is possible," Ethan replied, instilling in John a belief in his own untapped potential.

John's eyes sparkled with wonder as he launched the stone into the air. It disappeared momentarily, defying the limits of human perception, before returning to Earth with an impact, creating a far-reaching swell on the river's surface. The splash startled them, causing them both to lose their balance and tumble into the water.

Laughing and gasping for breath, they helped each other up, climbing up the bank, with Ethan retrieving a flopping fish that had been swept to the shore by the swell, gently returning it to the river.

"Didn't I say, let's not hurt the fish?" Ethan teased, their laughter filling the night air.

Surveying their surroundings, Ethan's gaze swept across the landscape, ensuring their playful mishap had gone unnoticed by prying eyes.

Turning to John, his expression softened with a sense of responsibility and care. He understood the significance of rest and preparation in the face of the challenges that awaited them.

"Let's head back," Ethan suggested, "We need to clean up, and you need to be well-rested for tomorrow's algebra test, John."

They gathered their belongings and prepared to make their way back through the woods.

With John's ethereal light leading the way, they ventured through the dense forest, their footsteps echoing softly amidst the tranquility of the night.

As they emerged from the darkness, nearing their house on Cleveland Street, a sense of accomplishment washed over them.

This evening's journey had been both physical and metaphysical. They knew that they were on the precipice of something extraordinary.

Entering their home, they quietly washed the mud from their clothing and slipped back into their rooms. Ethan's final thoughts before drifting off to sleep were of the endless possibilities that awaited John, and the immense responsibility he carried as his mentor.

Chapter 26

The school year was reaching its end, and as Ethan reflected on his accomplishments, he couldn't deny the satisfaction of excelling academically, despite the guilt of his knowledge of the future giving him an unfair advantage to complete research papers and fulfill the graduation requirements.

That day at school, he had made plans to meet up with George. It was a peculiar experience for him, mingling with teenagers almost half his age, but he understood the importance of maintaining appearances and fulfilling his role in this timeline.

"What are your plans for the summer?" Ethan enquired.

"Party, party my friend! Only a few weeks until graduation, and we're outta here!" George exclaimed with enthusiasm.

Ethan couldn't help but smile at George's energy. "It feels like this year has flown by, doesn't it?"

George, with a mischievous grin, playfully bumped fists with Ethan. "And mark my words, this summer,

I'm gonna reel in a bigger fish than you did last year!"

Ethan chuckled, aware of his modest fishing skills. "Well, I won't make it easy for you. We'll see who catches the trophy fish." Feeling some shame, in the knowledge that this was unlikely to occur.

George's eyes lit up with excitement. "Challenge accepted, Hollywood."

As they continued their conversation, George asked, "So, are we taking your Pops' car to Stacey's party down at the river tonight?"

Ethan hesitated for a moment before answering, "Not tonight, George. I promised John, I'd help him with his science project."

George nodded understandingly. "You're a good brother, Michael. I wish I had someone looking out for me like that."

Ethan gently placed his hand on George's shoulder, offering a comforting gesture. Deep down, Ethan knew that although George had a vibrant personality, his home life was often lonely. His parents were both hard workers, leaving little time for meaningful connection. It was a harsh contrast to the warm and loving atmosphere of the Miller family home.

As Ethan made his way through the high school playground, he couldn't help but notice the presence of one of the boys who had been tormenting John in recent weeks.

The boy briskly walked across the recreational area, heading towards John. Concerned about the possibility of an altercation, Ethan quickened his pace, ready to intervene if necessary.

Engaging in a physical confrontation was not his intention, as it would only demonstrate weakness among John's friends and classmates, potentially leading to further incidents.

As the boy approached John, Ethan's unease grew, fearing the worst. However, to his surprise and delight, the situation unfolded quite differently. John turned around, flashing a smile and asked, "How did you do, Josh?"

"Aced it, man! Your tips really helped," Josh replied with enthusiasm.

John beamed and said, "Glad I could help."

Josh continued the conversation, mentioning, "I've seen your performance in little league for Greenfield. Have you ever considered joining the school team?"

John's face lit up as he responded, "Definitely! Do you think I'd make the cut?"

"You've got my vote. I'll put in a good word with the coach. Are you heading out now?" Josh inquired.

"In a bit. I'm meeting up with my brother," John answered.

"Well, have a great weekend. See you on Monday, and make sure to sign up. We need someone with your pitching skills representing us at the finals!" Josh exclaimed.

Overhearing the entire exchange, Ethan felt a surge of reassurance. With each passing day, John's abilities became more apparent, and this particular situation could have easily taken a different turn.

Spotting his brother, John waved with a smile, and Ethan nodded in acknowledgment, responding, "I see you, Brother!"

Chapter 27

That evening, Ethan had the privilege of borrowing Michael Senior's prized possession, his Ranch Green 1978 Buick Skylark, for a special drive with John.

As they prepared to embark on their journey, Michael Senior settled into the passenger seat, offering valuable advice on how to handle the clutch.

"Remember to downshift as you approach the climb to the tower. It's steep, and you don't want to stall or slide backward," he shared, confident in his son's capabilities.

"Got it. Thanks for letting me borrow it, Dad," Ethan expressed gratefully, exchanging a warm glance with Mr. Miller.

"After the year you've had, you've more than proven yourself to us, son. Now go and have some fun!" Mr. Miller exclaimed cheerfully as he stepped out of the vehicle, with John eagerly joining him.

Ethan ignited the Skylark, the V6 engine awaking with a thunderous growl.

As he flicked on the car stereo, the electrifying sounds of Boston's debut album erupted from the speakers, filling the car with pulsating rock 'n' roll energy.

With the gears engaged, they smoothly glided away from the driveway, Janeane and Michael Senior waving them off as they embarked on their adventure down Cleveland Street.

Making a quick detour on their way to the tower, they swung by a nearby diner to grab milkshakes and burgers for their evening.

John leaned out of the window, relishing the feeling of the breeze against his face, as if he were the epitome of cool, cruising alongside his older brother.

"Hey, John, why don't you play one of your awesome mixtapes?" Ethan suggested.

John flipped the cassettes, and "Livin' On A Prayer" by Bon Jovi filled the car with exhilaration.

"Bon Jovi, great choice, love a bit of hair metal, John!" Ethan exclaimed, expressing his genuine admiration for John's selection. John grinned from ear to ear as they continued onwards with their journey.

Upon reaching Poet's Seat Tower, a popular landmark in Greenfield, Ethan and John reclined on the hood of the Skylark, basking in the soothing rays of the setting sun.

The familiar landscape unfolded before them, matching Ethan's vivid recollections.

To one side, the panoramic expanse stretched beyond the Connecticut River valley. On the other side, they beheld the visible landmarks, such as the hospital and sportsground. And during the winter months, when the foliage had shed its leaves, the outline of Route 5, the prominent highway connecting Greenfield, would come into view, tracing its path through the town.

Unbeknownst to John, this was a spot Ethan had frequently ventured to with Nicole, and it held special significance as the very place where he had proposed to her at the top of the tower, after an unforgettable hike.

As the sun disappeared over the horizon, the sky transformed into a canvas of twinkling stars. Ethan reached into the car, flicking on the stereo to blast John's favorite mixtape at full volume. Def Leppard's "Hysteria" echoed through the hills, adding to the magical atmosphere.

Ethan gazed at the vast expanse of the night sky, testing a theory, his finger extended towards the North Star.

"Can you isolate the power from a single star and

harness its energy?" he inquired, curiosity brimming in his voice.

John turned his attention to the star Ethan pointed at; his eyes fixated on its distant glow. As he focused his body ignited with a luminous glow, as if he had absorbed the star's energy. Heat radiated from him, creating a noticeable warmth in the air. A crackling static charge danced around him. And suddenly the engine beneath them roared to life!

Ethan couldn't contain his excitement and burst into laughter, his eyes sparkling with delight. The cosmic spectacle before them was nothing short of extraordinary. John's aura gradually returned to its normal state, and he turned to his brother with a mischievous grin.

"You mean, like that?" John asked, a playful tone in his voice.

Ethan nodded, unable to hide his smile. "Just like that," he replied, a sense of awe mingling with his amusement.

Taking in the breath-taking view, Ethan spoke again, his voice filled with a sense of hope. "You know, one day I'll move out and start a new chapter of my life. When that happens, I need you to step up and take care of Mom and Dad.

You'll be the man of the house, responsible for the

little things like taking out the trash and helping Mom with the chores."

John looked across at his brother, his eyes filled with admiration and determination. "I understand, Mike. Family is the most important thing. I'll be there for Mom and Dad. And I'll always use my abilities for the greater good, just like you taught me."

Ethan smiled, a sense of relief washing over him. He knew he could trust John to carry on the legacy they had built together.

Ethan turned to John, his eyes filled with wisdom and understanding. "Life can send us off our intended paths, leaving us feeling lost," he said, his voice steady. John absorbing his brother's words, sensing their significance.

"But here's the truth," Ethan continued, his conviction evident. "These moments don't define us. We have the power to rise above our past and become better versions of ourselves. We are not bound by our yesterdays; we can transcend them."

John felt a surge of determination, knowing he held the ability to shape his own future.

"We're not confined by past mistakes," Ethan emphasized, meeting John's gaze. "We can navigate life's challenges beyond our yesterdays and create our own path."

They turned their attention back to the starlit sky, spending hours talking about their shared passions for movies, music, and baseball. The bond between them grew even stronger as they cherished this moment of brotherhood and connection.

In that serene moment, surrounded by the beauty of the universe, Ethan found deliverance in knowing that he had prepared John for the challenges that lay ahead. The night sky became a symbol of endless possibilities.

Chapter 28

The first Saturday of July, the Miller family arrived at Wendy's Diner off Federal Street to celebrate the achievements of both children throughout the school year.

Upon entering the establishment, a friendly waitress guided them to their booth, and the air became infused with the aroma of sizzling bacon and the scent of freshly brewed coffee. In the corner, a jukebox played upbeat tunes, adding to the lively atmosphere.

Once seated at the table, they engaged in lively conversation, discussing their busy week. Michael Senior took the opportunity to congratulate his children on their report cards. Laughter and chatter filled the air, blending harmoniously with the bustling sounds of the diner. Michael wore a baseball jersey and cap, proudly displaying his love for the game, while John sported a Superman t-shirt, showcasing his admiration for his favorite superhero.

Following the arrival of their food order, the family indulged in the delicious offerings before them. They savored each bite of fluffy pancakes and crispy bacon, relishing the flavors and textures.

Michael Senior, with his distinguished moustache and warm smile, entertained the table with captivating stories from his days at the bank. His anecdotes sparked amusement among the family members. Janeane, always an elegant and nurturing presence, attentively listened to her husband's tales, occasionally offering gentle words of admiration to him.

Michael Senior smiling at his son, Michael "So, how was the baseball practice yesterday? Any home runs?"

"Yeah Dad, John hit a couple! The team is doing great this season."

A proud Mrs. Miller injected her enthusiasm "That's wonderful, John! I always knew you had a natural talent for sports."

They continued their meal, sharing stories of the past week, appreciating the simple pleasures of life.

Ethan excused himself from the table with a proud smile, his eyes meeting John's across the table.

As he strolled towards the restroom, he couldn't help but hum along to the befitting song playing in the background 'Finally Found A Home', by Huey Lewis & The News, feeling a sense of joy and contentment in this moment of togetherness.

As he finished washing his hands, the door swung open, revealing an elderly lady in a colorful dress with a floral pattern, entering the restroom.

He turned towards her with a polite smile. "Excuse me, miss," he said courteously, "the ladies' restroom is across the hall." The lady looked up at him, returning the smile, her eyes were filled with a sense of knowing.

In that moment, a mixture of relief and hesitation washed over Ethan as he brushed past her and made his way back into the hallway. His gaze settled on the Millers, seated at the breakfast table, engaged in lively conversation.

Sensing Ethan's emotional turmoil, she stepped beside him, offering a comforting presence. Her voice carried reassurance as she spoke, "They're going to be okay, Ethan."

Ethan, met her gaze and replied, "I know, and thank you."

"It is time," she stated calmly.

Taking one last look at the family he had briefly become a part of, the family he had yearned to belong to as a child, he returned to the men's restroom, opening the door and glancing back at the lady. "I'm ready," he declared before closing the door behind him.

Chapter 29

Having been discovered by another patron of the establishment, emergency medical services were promptly summoned from Baystate Franklin Medical Centre.

Michael was pronounced dead upon their arrival.

Subsequent medical examination revealed a diagnosis of a cerebral aneurysm, a condition characterized by the weakening and subsequent rupture of a blood vessel in the brain.

The attending physician at the hospital reassured the bereaved family that his passing would have been immediate and devoid of discomfort. Providing a semblance of comfort amid their overwhelming sorrow.

Chapter 30

Michael Miller's service took place at All Souls Church, on the corner of Main and Hope Street.

As the mourners came together to pay their respects, John Miller, stood before the gathered crowd.

With a trembling voice, John spoke of the wisdom and guidance that Michael had imparted upon him throughout their lives. John shared cherished memories, highlighting the profound impact his brother had on shaping his character and teaching him valuable life lessons.

Following John, George, took to the altar, ready to share heartfelt memories of their enduring friendship. His gaze shifted towards the grieving Miller family, particularly John, whom he had vowed to protect in Michael's absence.

With tearful animation, George portrayed a colorful narrative of their unbreakable bond, evoking both smiles and tears from the captivated crowd.

The service was not just a moment of mourning but also a celebration of Michael's life.

Through heartfelt stories and shared experiences, friends and family members painted a vivid picture of his vibrant personality, infectious laughter, and unwavering love for those around him.

After the funeral, George approached John amidst the melancholic gathering, extending an invitation to revisit the secret fishing spots he and John's late brother had frequented. It was a gesture of camaraderie, a heartfelt attempt to fill the void left by the departed. John's heart swelled with gratitude, touched by George's gesture of friendship and the promise of shared memories of Michael.

As they stood there, surrounded by mournful whispers and heavy hearts, John contemplated the thought of opening up to George, entrusting him with his secret.

The night at the tower echoed in John's mind, the poignant words that had been spoken to him. They carried the essence of his brother's wisdom, a guiding light in the darkness of grief.

He understood that while loss brought immense pain, there was also a profound beauty in honoring the departed, in cherishing the memories they left behind.

In the face of such loss, the Miller family found strength in the bonds of love and support they had cultivated.

The outpouring of love from their community helped carry them through the difficult days, reminding them that they were not alone in their grief.

Together, they leaned on each other, finding comfort and resilience in the unity of their family.

Chapter 31

It was a calm and clear Monday evening and Ethan sat on his usual bus ride home from the practice, the daylight fading into darkness.

The bus halted at Beacon Street Junction, and a distinguished gentleman in his fifties boarded. The bus was crowded, except for the empty seat beside Ethan. With a raised hand, Ethan signaled the vacant spot, and the man took a seat.

"Thank you," the man said, settling beside Ethan. Despite the digital age, he pulled out an old cassette player from his pocket and pressed the stop button. He pointed towards the night sky, where stars sparkled above.

"Beautiful, aren't they?" he remarked.

Ethan nodded in agreement. "Yes, very."

After a contemplative silence, the man spoke again. "When I was young, my brother and I used to spend hours gazing at the stars at night. That bright one over there is the North Star."

"Polaris," Ethan interjected.

"Exactly," the man replied.

Noticing Ethan's eyes on the cassette player on his lap, the man spoke.

"Ah, mixtapes, my friend, a lost art form. Back in the day, we used to pour our hearts into creating the perfect mix for someone special," he said, his eyes twinkling with memories.

Ethan's face lit up with understanding. "Absolutely! I used to lose myself for hours, carefully curating playlists for different moods and occasions."

The man nodded appreciatively. "You've got it, young man. Music has a way of touching our souls like nothing else. By the way, what were you listening to?" he asked, noticing Ethan's earbuds.

Ethan smiled and shared, "Steely Dan, their early stuff."

As the bus passed by Wendy's diner, the man's eyes sparkled. "Ah, Steely Dan, the good stuff!" he exclaimed, pressing the button to signal his upcoming stop. The bus slowed down and halted at the corner of Leonard Street. The gentleman rose from his seat.

"It was a pleasure meeting you, young man. I hope to cross paths again. My friends call me Johnny," he said, his voice filled with warmth.

Returning the smile, Ethan replied, "Likewise, Johnny.

I am Ethan, and I look forward to it."

As Johnny made his way to the front of the bus, bidding the driver farewell with a gentle nod, "Goodnight, Bobby."

"Goodnight, Mr. Miller," the driver responded warmly.

The bus continued its journey, while Ethan sat there, contemplating the encounter with John Miller.

There was something magical about their brief reconnection, a sense that the threads of time had intentionally intertwined to bring them back together.

Chapter 32

Ethan disembarked the bus at Olive Street and continued his journey home.

Having turned the corner onto Hope Street, he spotted Nicole standing by the porch, bathed in the warm glow of the porch light.

Paint splatters adorned her jeans and top, evidence of their recent bathroom renovation project. Her eyes shimmered with tears. He rushed to her concerned that something had happened. The moment she caught sight of him emerging from the darkness, her face transformed into a brilliant smile.

In that magical instant, Ethan pointed to Nicole's belly. A sparkle appeared in her eyes, and happiness spread across her face.

Their embrace was filled with a deep sense of connection, knowing that their love had created new life, their journey together expanding into the realm of parenthood.

About The Author

Within his personal journey, Simon's love for research writing and the power of music has always been a great source of inspiration to him.

In the quiet and private moments, a creation began to take shape—'Beyond Our Yesterdays.'

Residing in the town of Guildford, England, Simon finds serenity in the embrace of his loving family and their loyal canine companion.

Through his captivating stories, Simon effortlessly transcends the ordinary, forging genuine connections with his audience.